Nia and the Kingdoms of Celebration

Written by Philip Robinson

Illustrated by Cherise Harris

Acknowledgements

Thanks to Nicole, my wife, and kids for giving me the space to complete this book. They inspired and encouraged, reminding me why we celebrate and why we sing.

It was a pleasure working with Cherise Harris from Barbados. She is a wonderful artist and I look forward to working with her again in the future.

Thanks to Sean Brown, who was the first person to give me thorough feedback on an early draft of this book.

To Judith Burns and the 2016 class 8A1 at Bangor Academy and Sixth Form College in Northern Ireland, my humble gratitude for your written feedback. Thanks to Emily M, Evan C, Evie O, Isaac C, Jack D, Jack M, Jake H, Joshua F, Kirstin T, Kristian T, Lewis H, Logan B, Lois C, Lois L, Lucy B, Lucy P, Luke B, Megan H, Morgan M, Sophie T, Stephen D, Taylor N and Tori-lee B.

To my colleagues and friends who [never] grew tired of hearing me talk about this book and bombard them with pictures and updates, here it is. Thanks for your belief in me!

First published by Kingdoms of Celebration Publishing in 2017

@kingdomsofcelebration

Copyright © 2017 Philip Robinson

Edited by Joanna Robinson

ISBN: 978-1-9998923-0-2

KINGDOMS OF CELEBRATION PUBLISHING

Nia and the
Kingdoms of Celebration

For Nadrianne, Rachel and Sara

When you see this symbol, it is a good
point in the story to take a break and
celebrate bedtime. Pleasant dreams!

*M*any years ago the Earth was one land. There were five different kingdoms but no borders, fences or separation by water. People looked, talked, dressed and lived differently, depending on their kingdom of origin. This was perhaps the happiest time on Earth.

Together, the kingdoms became known as the *Kingdoms of Celebration*. But they were not always known by that name.

In the north was the *Kingdom of Precious Metals and Stones* and in the south was the *Kingdom of Birds*. In the west was the *Kingdom of Seashells* and in the east was the *Kingdom of Lights*. There was just one more...

At the centre of the Earth was the *Kingdom of Fragrant Flowers*. Its people were known as the *Fragranti*. Here lived Princess Nia, daughter of King Kani and Queen Malia.

Princess Nia was very beautiful. Her skin was dark like the bark of the cassia tree and glowed as though the sun's rays lived in her cheeks. Nia spent most of her days in the Ipakati Gardens, at the heart of the kingdom, playing among the flowers, enjoying their colours and smells. One day King Kani whispered to her, "Nia, it is good to play, but, remember, someday you will be a leader in our kingdom."

"Me? A leader?" Nia chuckled, continuing to fix tiny, multicoloured geraniums in her black, curly hair. She loved her hair. Some days it was tightly braided like the vines of the honeysuckle, while other days it looked like loose bunches of dagga flowers styled by the wind.

"Yes Nia, a leader," the queen affirmed, readjusting the geraniums in Nia's hair. "Just like you know the flowers, you need to know our neighbours, their flags, their customs, their dreams and desires."

So Nia travelled often to the other kingdoms with her parents, accompanied by the Elders, who knew everything about anything. These journeys were long and tiring with much to learn. Yet the princess looked forward to these trips as she found new friends in each kingdom who shared her spirit of adventure and fun. She would always find chances to slip away with them and play.

Nia enjoyed the mysterious caves and mountains of the North, the windswept hills and forests of the South, the rolling waves of the West and the dazzling lights of the East. Yet she always longed for home and the sights and smells of her beloved flowers.

When not travelling, Nia took every chance she could to run to the Ipakati Gardens with the other Fragranti children. This was especially joyous during the planting of the rainbow roses, which only bloomed at the start of the wet season.

"What colour roses will we see this season?" the children debated. "Red!" "Orange!" "Yellow!" most suggested. "Err, terror… cows?" hesitated a younger boy. "Huh?" exclaimed the other children. "Turquoise!" they corrected in unison. The boy looked embarrassed but he soon joined in the laughter.

"Well I can't wait until the first rose opens!" declared Nia. "According to the Elders, each unopened rose is a promise waiting for its moment." Nia was always attentive to the Elders, especially when they talked about the flowers. "Have you heard the new song of the rainbow roses?" Nia did not wait for a response and burst into song:

"Rainbow roses fill the fields with colours that we've never seen.
Brightly blooming everywhere, the roses' fragrance fills the air.

Celebration! Celebration!
Hearts and hands we now unite;
Celebration! Celebration!
Like the roses fill the night"

Later that day, Nia walked with her parents around the kingdom. The anticipation of the rainbow roses was evident, as music filled the air, like the sweet fragrance of magnolias.

"I wonder how my new friends in the other kingdoms celebrate the rainbow roses," Nia pondered aloud.

"They don't," King Kani abruptly replied. "Each kingdom is unique," he continued. "The roses only grow in our kingdom. This is our celebration."

Nia's head and shoulders drooped and her eyes hazed with disappointment and doubt.

Queen Malia's heart sank as she saw the sparkle disappear from her daughter's eyes. The queen flashed a sudden smile as an idea sparked in her mind.

"What if we invited your new friends and all the kingdoms to us?" suggested Malia. "They could all come see and smell the roses!" she continued. "I'm thinking, flowers everywhere, loads of music, good food and one big party."

The queen loved parties, as did Kani, but he tried his best not to let it show. With a calm, stately posture, he responded,

"I guess it's what a leader would do."

Princess Nia squealed with delight.

"Yes, yes, yes! I can't wait to see their faces!"

At the next sunrise, the runners, the fastest, fittest messengers in the land, were set to journey to the other four kingdoms, delivering invitations to the 'Celebration of the Rainbow Roses'.

Princess Nia appeared scampering with four small packets in her hands. "Wait! Wait!" she beckoned.

"Hello Princess, are you ok?" the runners asked, startled by her sudden appearance. "I'm fine," panted Nia, as she tried to catch her breath. "Can you please also take these rainbow seeds to my friends?"

King Kani, approaching to give the runners final instructions and well-wishes, overheard his daughter's request.

"Nia, these seeds never grow beyond our kingdom."

"I know, Father," Nia replied. "But what if their moment is still to come?" As the king recognised these words from the Elders, he had no response. "Very well," he said, nodding slowly toward the runners, as Nia gleefully handed over the packets of seeds.

"Now, great runners of the Fragranti," proclaimed King Kani. "Be swift, be strong, be sure that love leads you!" Then he and Nia watched as the runners disappeared in four different directions.

Many moons passed as the Fragranti prepared for the Celebration of the Rainbow Roses. The kingdom looked more resplendent than ever before, with many brightly-coloured flowers made into decorations.

"Come on, come on! Let's get this done before that dark cloud of rain arrives!" ordered the chief designer, a lady with a most elaborate hairstyle. "I know, I know, you can't get your hair wet," replied one of the men cheekily. He quickly stopped grinning as his eyes met her unamused stare.

Princess Nia came running with another handful of flowers from the garden. "Do you need anymore? What colours do we need now? Should I stir that for you? Oh, I can do that!"

"There's plenty to do, Princess," responded the chief designer, replacing the flowers in Nia's plaited hair. "But you children have done enough for the day, which is more than I can say for some!" she continued, glaring at the man who had dared to comment on her hair earlier. Nia giggled. She loved her people and their ways.

But the chief designer was right. Nia was exhausted. She soon found herself resting against a giant Baobab tree, where she drifted into a deep sleep and a world of dreams.

Nia dreamed of Kat from the northern Kingdom of Precious
Metals and Stones. They played and dressed up with sparkling
jewellery. Bracelets and necklaces made of diamond, gold and silver
glistened in the gentle rays of sunshine. Kat spoke of rumbling
caves, full of jewels, and mysterious tunnels, deep beneath the
kingdom, where one day they would bravely explore and find
treasure of their own.

The princess' dreams floated to the southern Kingdom of Birds. She was standing at the top of a hill with her friend Cheona. They wore wings of fine golden feathers on their backs and outstretched their arms, as though they were ready to fly. Down a hill and across a green, open field, the girls zipped and squealed as the wind filled their wings. Cheona led her to a forest. It was dark. But the dancing of the trees in the wind and the sound of many birds singing, chirping, whistling, flitting and swooping all at once, made the forest seem bright and alive.

She then dreamed of Arun from the eastern Kingdom of Lights. Fireworks banged and lit up a dusky sky. Arun stomped around making a roaring sound, while stuffing his mouth with his favourite snack of hot chili peppers. He tried to convince Nia that he was really a fire-breathing dragon. Nia began to believe him.

But as Arun was about to release fiery flames, the princess found herself bobbing in the ocean. Her dreams transported her to the western Kingdom of Seashells, where her friends, the twins, Mai and Miko, suddenly appeared from beneath the water's surface.

With smiles, the twins called for her to swim further and dive deeper. Then, with deep breaths, they disappeared.

As Nia waited for the twins to reappear in her dream, she felt chilly water slapping against her face and heard a loud "BOOM! RUMBLE! CRASH! SPLASH!" like waves surging and lashing against the cliffs.

"Come Nia! We must go now!" came the distressed voice of Queen Malia, tugging her arm and waking her from her dreams.

"Wha...what's going on?" Nia mumbled and trembled in confusion. She awoke to the sight of gloom, scattered decorations, gusting winds and torrents of pelleting rainfall.

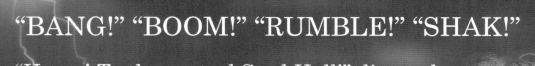

"BANG!" "BOOM!" "RUMBLE!" "SHAK!"

"Hurry! To the central Seed Hall!" directed King Kani, pointing the way to their strongest shelter.

The Fragranti frantically fled for fear. Their homes were being destroyed as a mighty storm and earthquake intensified, causing the land to crack, flood and break apart.

"BOOM!" "BOOM!"

"CRACKLE!" "POW!"

A distant volcano erupted, sending billows of dark smoke and ash toward the kingdom.

"Why is this happening?" asked Princess Nia, clinging tightly to her mother.

"This is just nature, my precious petal," replied the queen. "Like all seasons this will pass."

But not all the Fragranti felt comforted and convinced that this was just nature at work. Never before had all of nature's forces combined to wreak such devastation.

They became suspicious of the other kingdoms.

Nia listened to murmurs of blame and conspiracy around the Seed Hall.

"Could it be the northern kingdom's mining causing the earth to quake and mountains to crumble?"

"Yes, but remember, the eastern kingdom are always trying to create bigger, brighter, more explosive fireworks. Maybe they succeeded."

"Well, you can be sure that the southern kingdom will be out testing their wings with these strong winds."

"As will the western kingdom. They are bound to be happy with these rising floods. 'More water, more waves,' they say."

The mood of the Fragranti was desperate. The Seed Hall shook with each tremor and they feared it would not endure the storm.

"BLAM!" They were startled as a window was flung open by a strong gust. A bright flash of lightning allowed Princess Nia to glimpse the outline of someone running.

"Hey, I think I saw one of our runners!" Nia alerted, as she pushed her way to the window and got a clearer view of the runner returning from the east.

The runner arrived out of breath, saying, "King Kani, Queen Malia, I have delivered your invitation, but the Kingdom of Lights will not come to our party. The mountains that once sheltered their kingdom have crumbled, the rains are heavy and the winds are cold. They are building bigger fires to keep them warm."

"Quick! Open the door! There's another runner coming from the west!" someone frantically shouted, as they rushed to the western door to let the runner into the hall.

The runner, drenched and out of breath, arrived saying, "King Kani, Queen Malia, I have delivered your invitation but the Kingdom of Seashells will not come to our party. The cliffs are falling, giant waves are crashing and water is rising above their homes. They are building stronger boats to resist the waves!"

"What about the other runners?" lamented Queen Malia. "I'll check the south window, you take the north," directed King Kani. After a while a third runner was spotted approaching from the south, running so fast she could have been flying.

The runner arrived, caught her breath and then reported, "King Kani, Queen Malia, I have delivered your invitation but the Kingdom of Birds will not come to our party. The lightning has set their forests on fire, threatening their homes. They are following the birds further south!"

"Well everyone is saving themselves except us!" complained an angry man, emerging from the shadows. "He's right, we are doomed here hiding away in this storage hall," added another. "And there's still no sign of our northern runner!" he continued, pointing at the northern horizon lost behind a blanket of darkness.

King Kani, listening to the Fragranti grumble and watching their frightened faces in the glow of the torches, lifted his voice and said, "this is our darkest season yet, but, by being together, we have hope!" The Elders stepped into the light of the torches to support the king.

The Elders had this to say:

"Torches bring
light to the dark;
mighty birds
rule the wind;
cliffs withstand
the ocean's waves;
diamonds rest where
eruptions end.
The promise of hope is
our light,
It gives us
strength and wings;
This is why
we celebrate!
This is why
we sing!"

Princess Nia listened carefully to the Elders. She quietly repeated the phrase "this is why we sing" to herself, until she looked out to the fields and noticed, in spite of the storm, the rainbow roses were blooming.

The princess exclaimed, "this is why we sing!"

"THIS IS WHY WE SING!"

With that she quickly dashed through the doors of the great Seed Hall into the storm and toward the rainbow roses, before the king or queen could stop her

The princess ran through the stinging raindrops. She skipped over cracks and splashed through puddles. The loud BANGs and BOOMs still echoed but the words of the Elders were louder in her head. She was determined to reach the rainbow roses.

The other children, inspired by the princess, rushed after her, escaping their parents and shouting together,

"THIS IS WHY WE SING!"

Princess Nia, by now dripping from the rain and shivering in the wind, arrived at the Ipakati gardens. She slowly raised her hands toward the sky, caught her breath and sang:

"Rainbow roses fill the fields with colours that we've never seen!"

As the princess sang these words, all the roses, one by one, opened and uncurled like dancers waking from slumber. The other children, on seeing this, joined the princess, singing:

"Brightly blooming everywhere, the roses' fragrance fills the air!"

With more voices, the roses stretched wider and grew faster. Their stems became like tree trunks and their leaves like vast tents that shielded the people from the wind and rain.

"Come! Let's join our children! This is why we sing!" shouted Queen Malia, urging the awestruck parents to join in. They broke their silence and the noise was tremendous:

**"Celebration! Celebration!
Hearts and hands we now unite."**

"Celebration! Celebration!

Like the roses fill the night!"

The roses made one final reach for the skies then bent to intertwine their branches, forming a colourful canopy above the kingdom. This protected the Fragranti from the storm that continued to rage around them.

The BANGs and the BOOMs were still present, but the Fragranti were no longer afraid. The Elders spoke these words:

"Our princess, our children, sang with loud voice,

Reminding us fear is just one choice.

Come dark skies, quakes and heavy rainfall,

This flowery fortress is refuge for all!"

The dark skies, quakes and heavy rainfall continued for many moons. Yet they too had their season and gradually decreased until they ceased and peace returned to the kingdom.

The world was now a very different place. The quakes caused the earth to break and mountains to crumble. Water from the storm's floods filled cracks and valleys where mountains once stood. Streams became rivers and rivers became seas, separating lands and kingdoms, continents and countries.

"Wow, everything has changed," said Princess Nia to the King and Queen, as they walked along the new river flowing through the middle of the kingdom.

"Yes, but our love remains," smiled Queen Malia, picking fresh geraniums for the princess' hair. King Kani looked at his daughter with pride in his eyes and said, "you've certainly changed. You're now a leader." Nia smiled at her father and ran off to join the other children among the flowers.

But these peaceful days were disrupted one dawn by the sounds of "**BANG**" and "**BOOM**" from the distant, eastern horizon. Panic started to rise but quickly turned to excitement, as they listened closely to what was actually rhythmic, familiar and pleasant:

"BANG-BOOM-BA-BANG-BANG-BOOM!"

The sound drew closer and louder. Voices in song could now be heard. **"Rainbow roses fill the fields!"** they sang, appearing dressed in bright yellow, red and orange. It was the Kingdom of Lights arriving, with their flares, sparklers and joyous singing bright like the sunshine rising behind them. The Fragranti were astonished to see them and, moreover, to hear them singing their beloved song. They ran out to meet them and joined in the singing:

"Brightly blooming everywhere..."

But were interrupted by the sound of wind coming from the south.

With a "*whoosh, whoosh, whistle, hummmm,*" birds and kites appeared, swooping, circling and dancing in the air to the beat of the drum, with singing rising from beneath their wings:

"...the roses' fragrance fills the air!"

The southern Kingdom of Birds arrived with their colourful, feathery garments. The Fragranti were astounded. "Two kingdoms arriving singing our song? How could this be?"

But the wonders continued, as the sound of splashing waves stirred the gentle flow of a mist-covered river, newly formed to the west of the kingdom. Melodious voices rose like a tide from across the water, singing:

"Celebration! Celebration! Hearts and hands we now unite!"

Magnificent boats arrived carrying the western Kingdom of Seashells. They continued singing as they anchored along the river's banks.

There was still sadness in spite of the growing party. The northern runner had not returned. There was no sign from the north. King Kani invited those gathered to pause for a moment's silence, as all eyes looked northwards.

Then came the sound of distant horns, **"PAH-PA-PA-PAH"**, echoing from between the mountains. "Look! That's the flag of the northern kingdom!" announced someone. "Yes, but listen! Listen to what they sing!" exclaimed Nia.

> **"Celebration! Celebration! Like the roses fill the night!"**

And so arrived the Kingdom of Precious Metals and Stones. Ahead of them was the northern runner.

He beamed with joy.

He was finally home.

Princess Nia ran between the bustling crowds, searching for each of her friends. They laughed with excitement as they found each other, telling their stories at the same time. "I planted your seeds Nia," said Cheona. "And so did we," interjected the twins, Miko and Mai together. "The roses grew and grew until they covered our kingdom!" explained Arun, trying to stretch his arms wider than possible. By now everyone realised that they had all experienced the same miracle.

An Elder from the northern kingdom confirmed their story
and had this to say:

"Battered by the stormy rains,
trembling with each quake,
fear and shelter soon became
our only path to take.
Then we heard your voices
on the wind so strong —
flowers rose and shielded us
as you sang your song.
Now we're here to celebrate
all we thought was gone.
Beyond the force of
nature's might
is love that
makes us one."

They carried on as one for many days and nights. Queen Malia and King Kani watched their daughter with delight, as she played and laughed together with all of her friends. The sights and sounds of celebration were beautiful and varied, just like the colourful rainbow roses still in full bloom.

Some people sang, some shouted, some jumped on the spot, some twirled in circles, some stamped and kicked, while others just waved their hands in the air as though they had nothing to care about. This was what celebration looked like. This was when the kingdoms first became known as the *Kingdoms of Celebration*.

Princess Nia continued to blossom in beauty, bravery and wisdom.

She was a leader and went on to have many adventures with her new friends.

This was perhaps the happiest time on Earth.

We hope you enjoyed this story! Share feedback and find out more about Princess Nia's friends and their kingdoms at:

◊ facebook.com/kingdomsofcelebration

◊ instagram.com/kingdomsofcelebration

◊ Or write by email to kingdomsofcelebration@btinternet.com

15059595R00028

Printed in Great Britain
by Amazon